AMAZING MYSTERIES

MERMAIDS

BY ASHLEY GISH

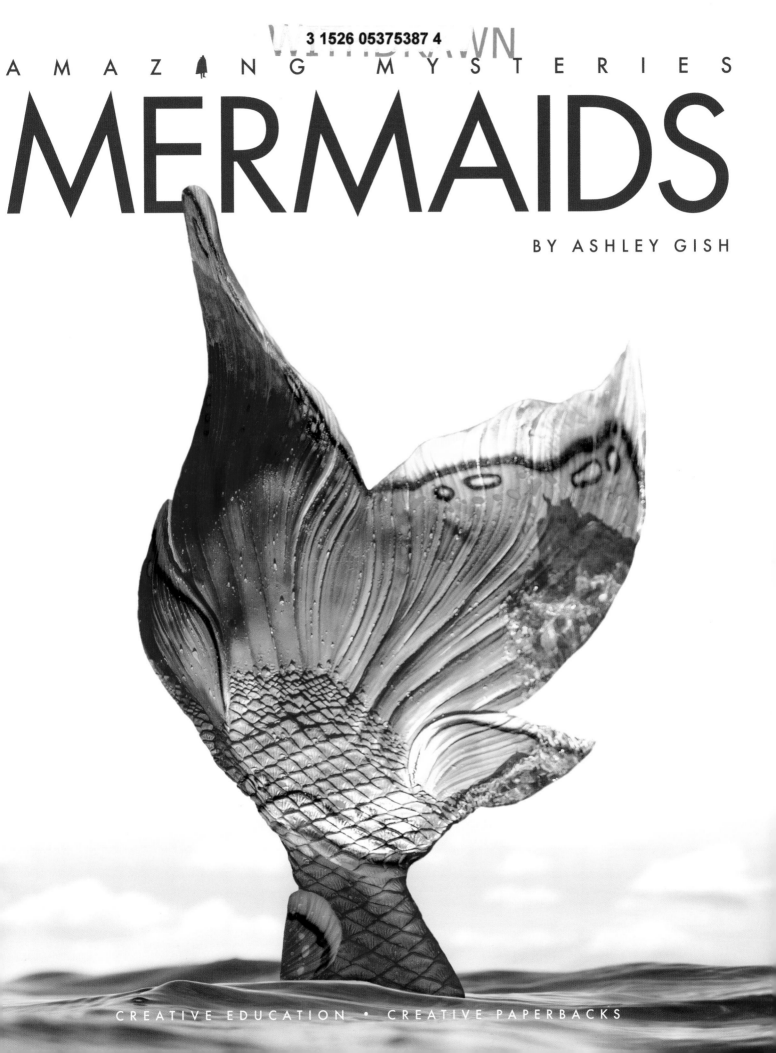

CREATIVE EDUCATION • CREATIVE PAPERBACKS

Published by Creative Education and Creative Paperbacks
P.O. Box 227, Mankato, Minnesota 56002
Creative Education and Creative Paperbacks are imprints of
The Creative Company
www.thecreativecompany.us

Design by The Design Lab
Production by Dana Koehler
Art direction by Rita Marshall
Printed in the United States of America

Photographs by Alamy (Heritage Image Partnership Ltd), Creative
Commons Wikimedia (Ministério da Cultura/Homologação do
tombamento de obras do Niemeyer, Witold Pruszkowski/National
Museum Kraków), Dreamstime (Nick Tamvakis), Getty Images
(Robbie Goodall/Moment, Zena Holloway), iStockphoto (borchee,
cdwheatley, duncan1890, Eerik, FG Trade, Jenhung Huang,
Rafinade, sc0rpi0nce, Yuri_Arcurs), SuperStock (Artepics/age
fotostock, Massimo Pizzotti/age fotostock)

Library of Congress Cataloging-in-Publication Data
Names: Gish, Ashley, author.
Title: Mermaids / Ashley Gish.
Series: Amazing mysteries.
Includes index.
Summary: A basic exploration of the appearance, behaviors, and
origins of mermaids, the aquatic mythological creatures known for
their singing. Also included is a story from folklore about how a
mermaid returned a beggar's kindness.
Identifiers:
ISBN 978-1-64026-219-5 (hardcover)
ISBN 978-1-62832-782-3 (pbk)
ISBN 978-1-64000-354-5 (eBook)
This title has been submitted for CIP processing under LCCN
2019937876.

First Edition HC 9 8 7 6 5 4 3 2 1
First Edition PBK 9 8 7 6 5 4 3 2 1

Table of Contents

Merfolk's hair, skin, and scales may vary in color and depend on their location.

Merfolk are **aquatic** creatures. They are half-human and half-fish. In place of legs, they have tails covered in **scales**. Females are called mermaids. Males are called mermen.

aquatic living or growing in water

scales small, thin plates that grow from the skin and typically overlap

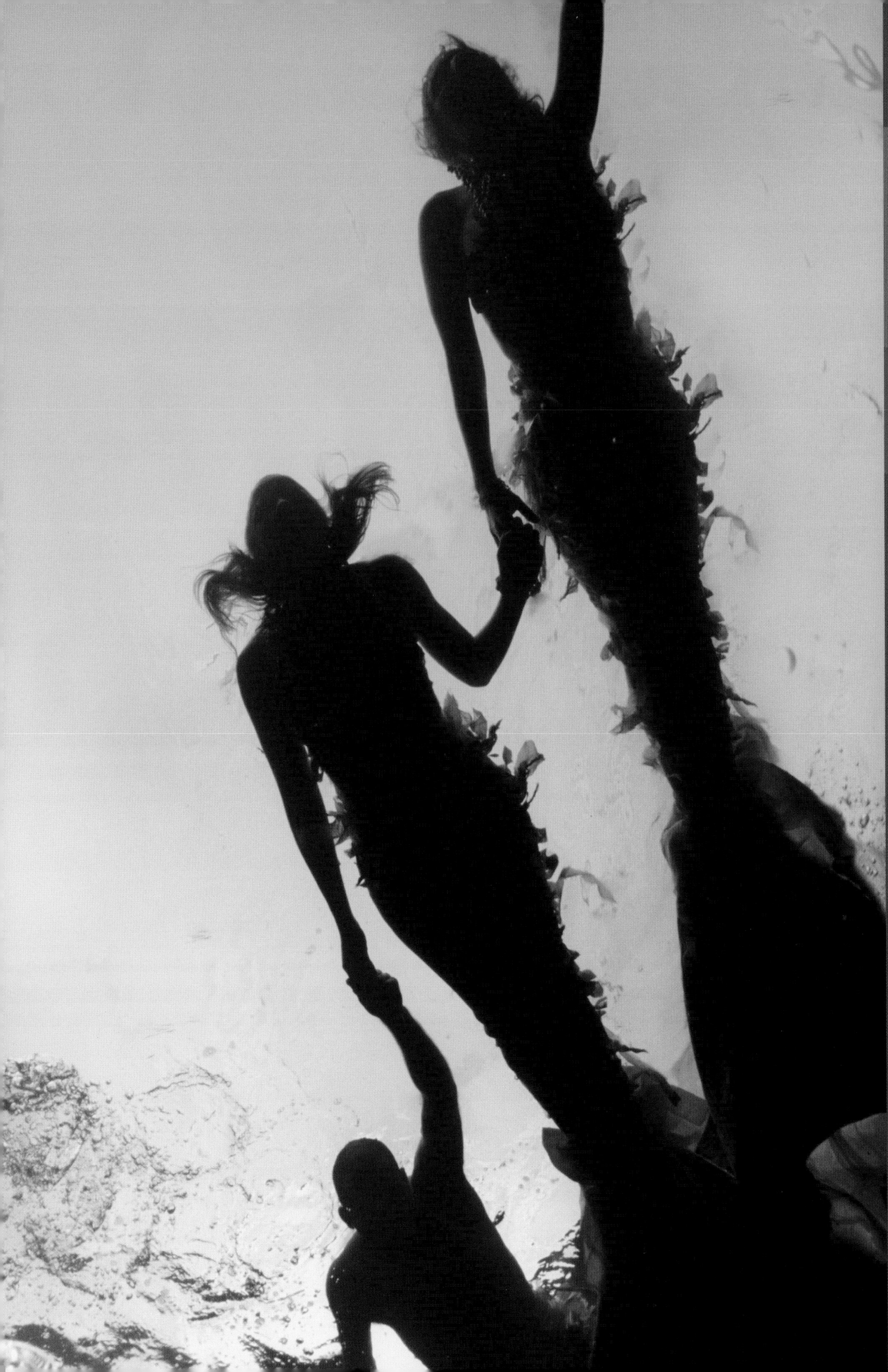

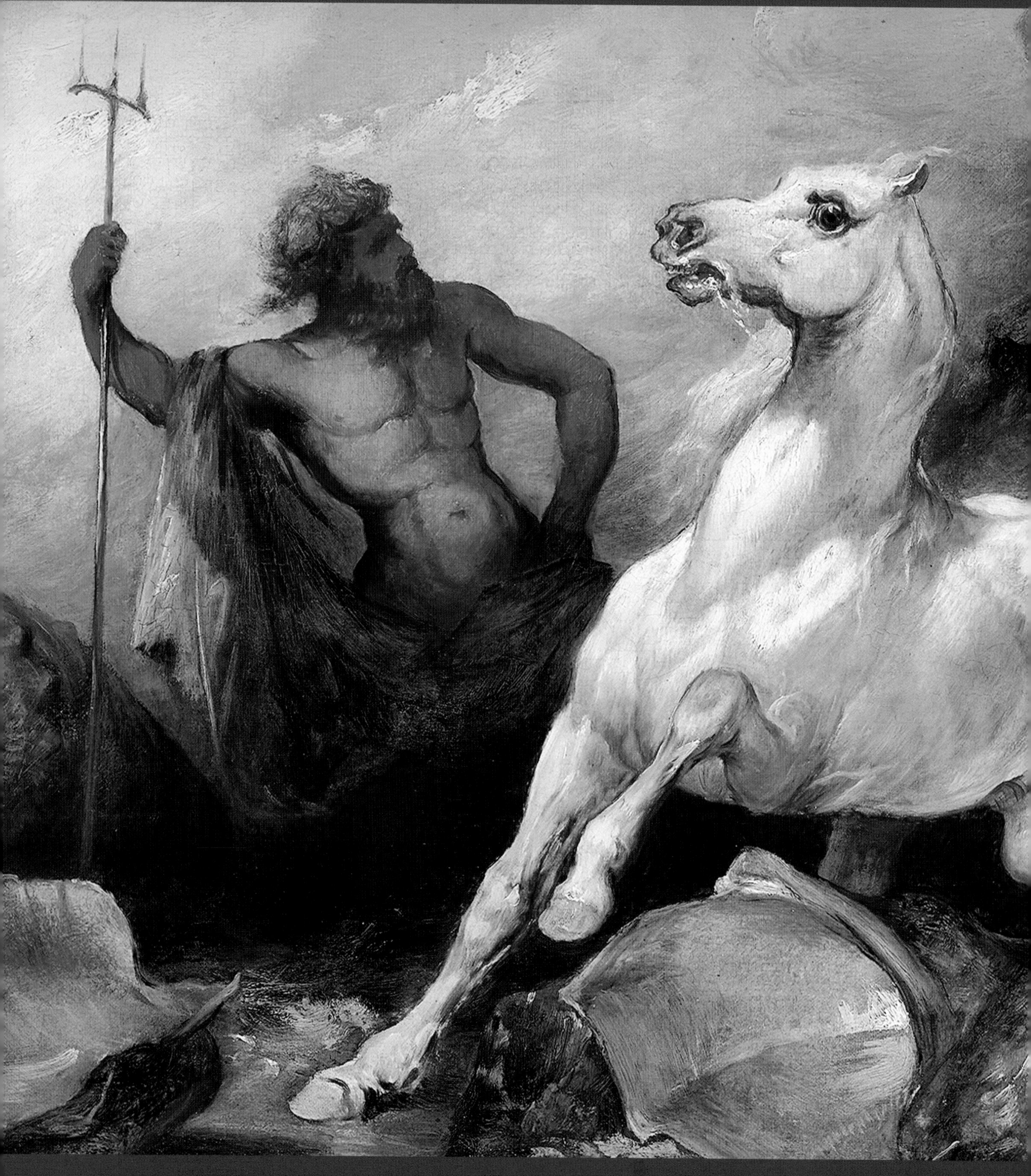

In Roman stories, Triton was a merman who carried a trident, or three-pointed spear.

The first stories about mermaids were told about 2,400 years ago. Many peoples have described similar creatures. Some, including sirens from Greek **mythology**, are related to mermaids.

mythology a collection of myths, or traditional beliefs or stories that explain how something came to be or that are about a person or object

Iara are often blamed for the disappearance of men in or near the Amazon.

Iara are mermaids who live in South America's Amazon River. Mondao live near **dams** in Africa. Mermaids have also been spotted around the Gulf Islands in British Columbia.

dams barriers built to hold back water

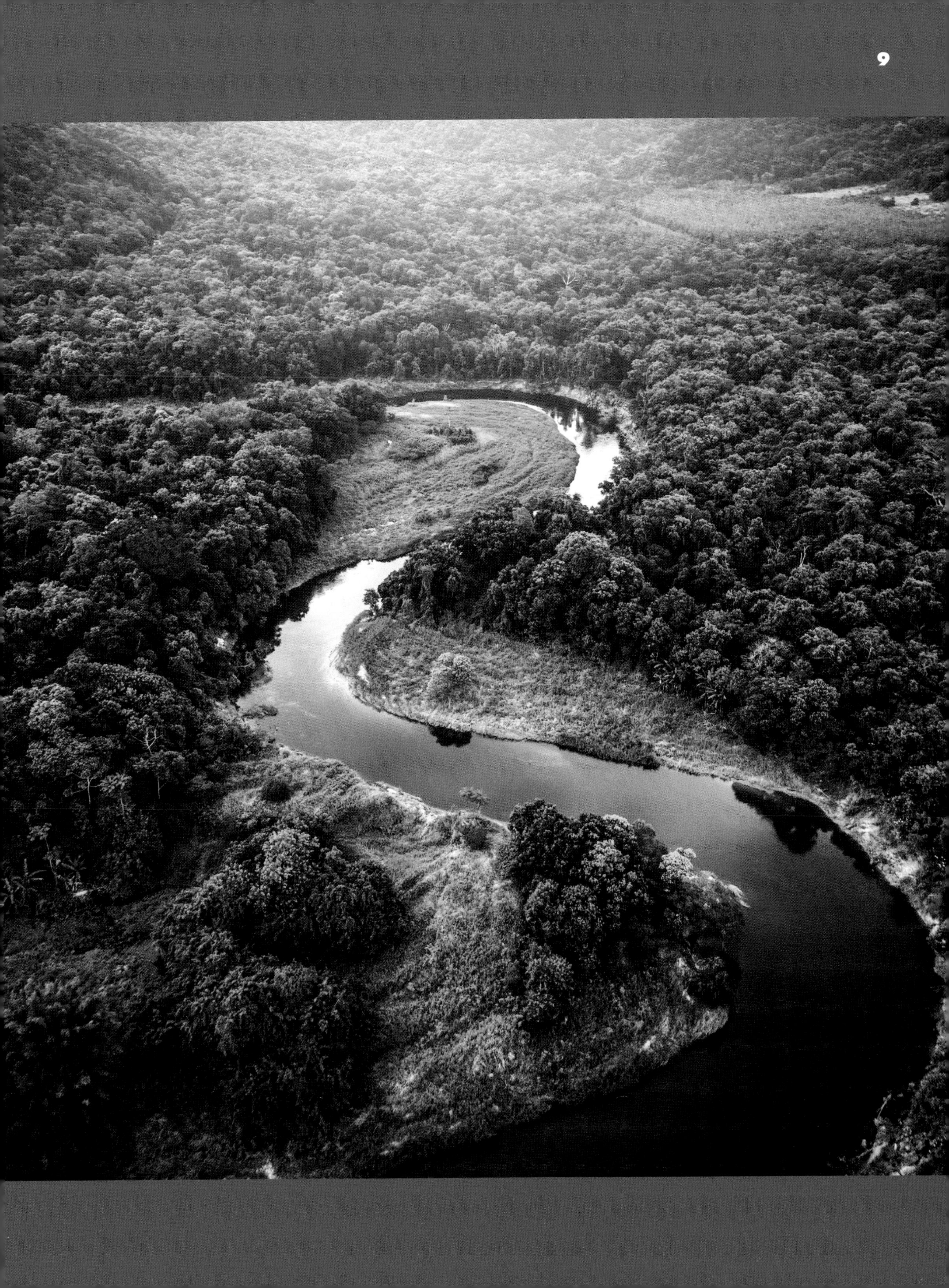

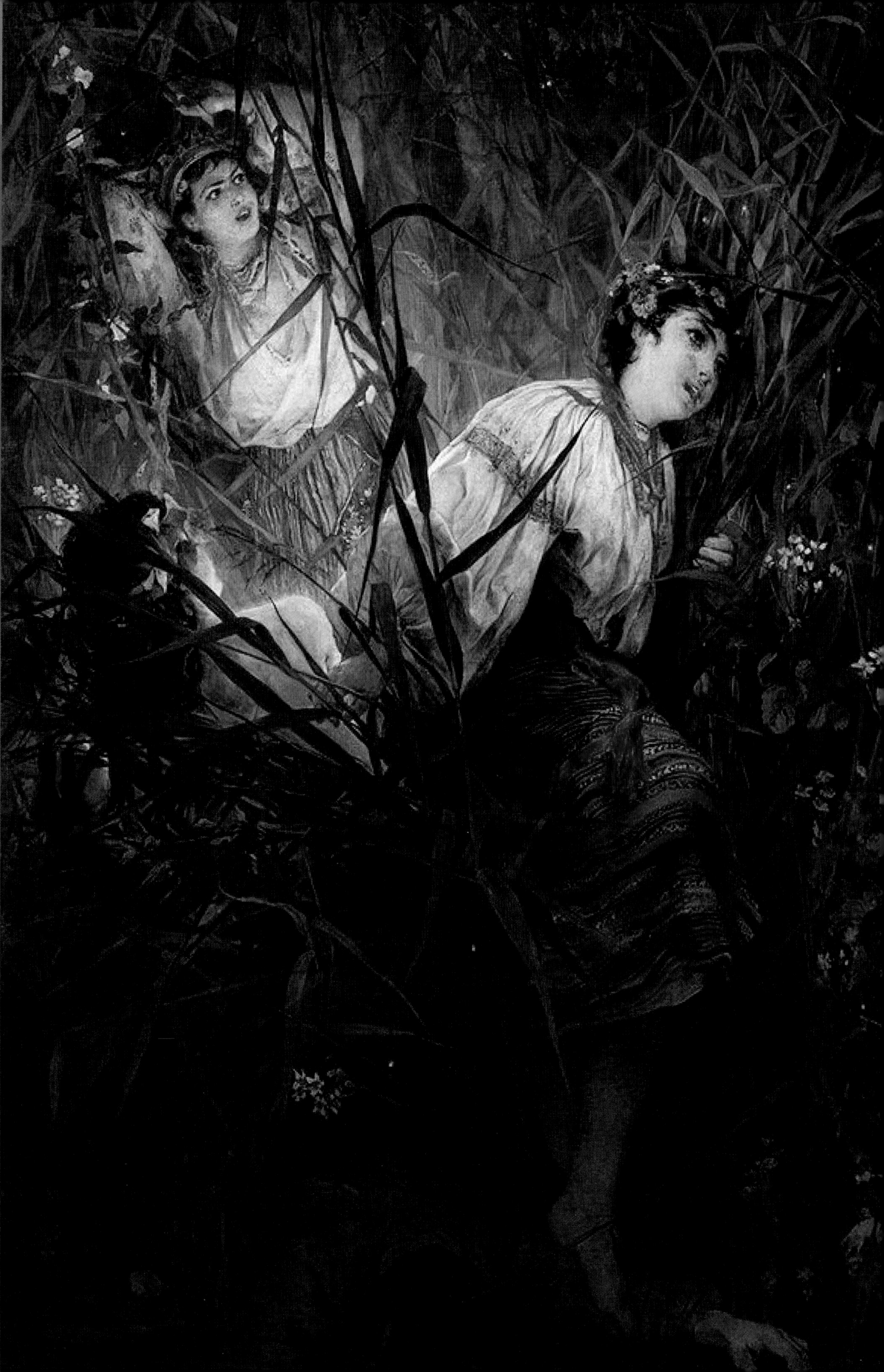

In Russia, rusalki have skin like cloudy glass. Though they live in rivers, they have legs and can walk on land. People often mistake rusalki for ghosts. In Japan, the ningyo has sharp teeth and horns.

Rusalki are believed to regularly come ashore to dance and climb trees.

Some mermaids move from place to place. Others live in deep underwater cities or near islands. Evil mermaids may live alone in caves. They can change forms to become sea snakes.

For hundreds of years, people thought unfamiliar sea animals were mermaids.

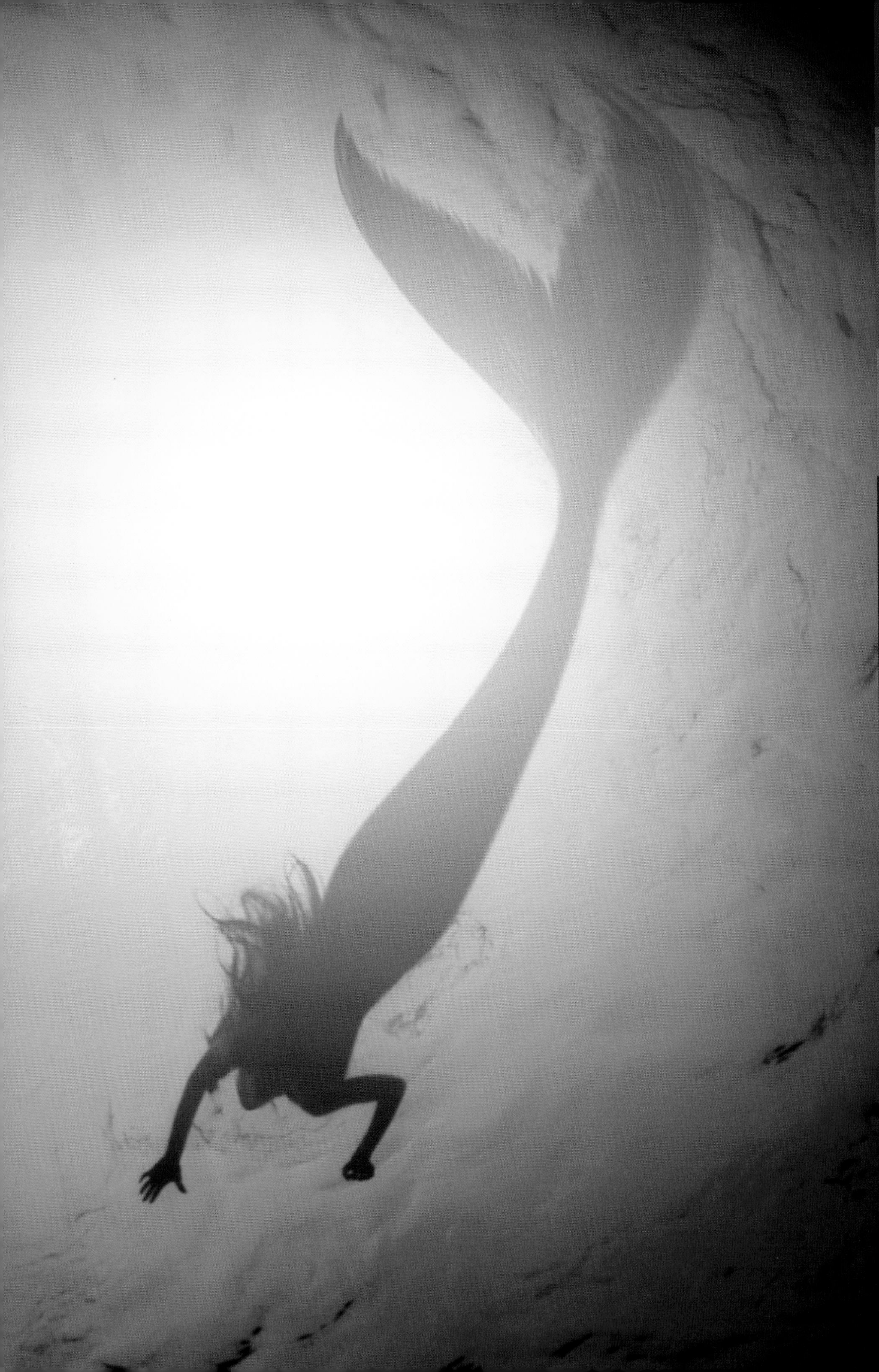

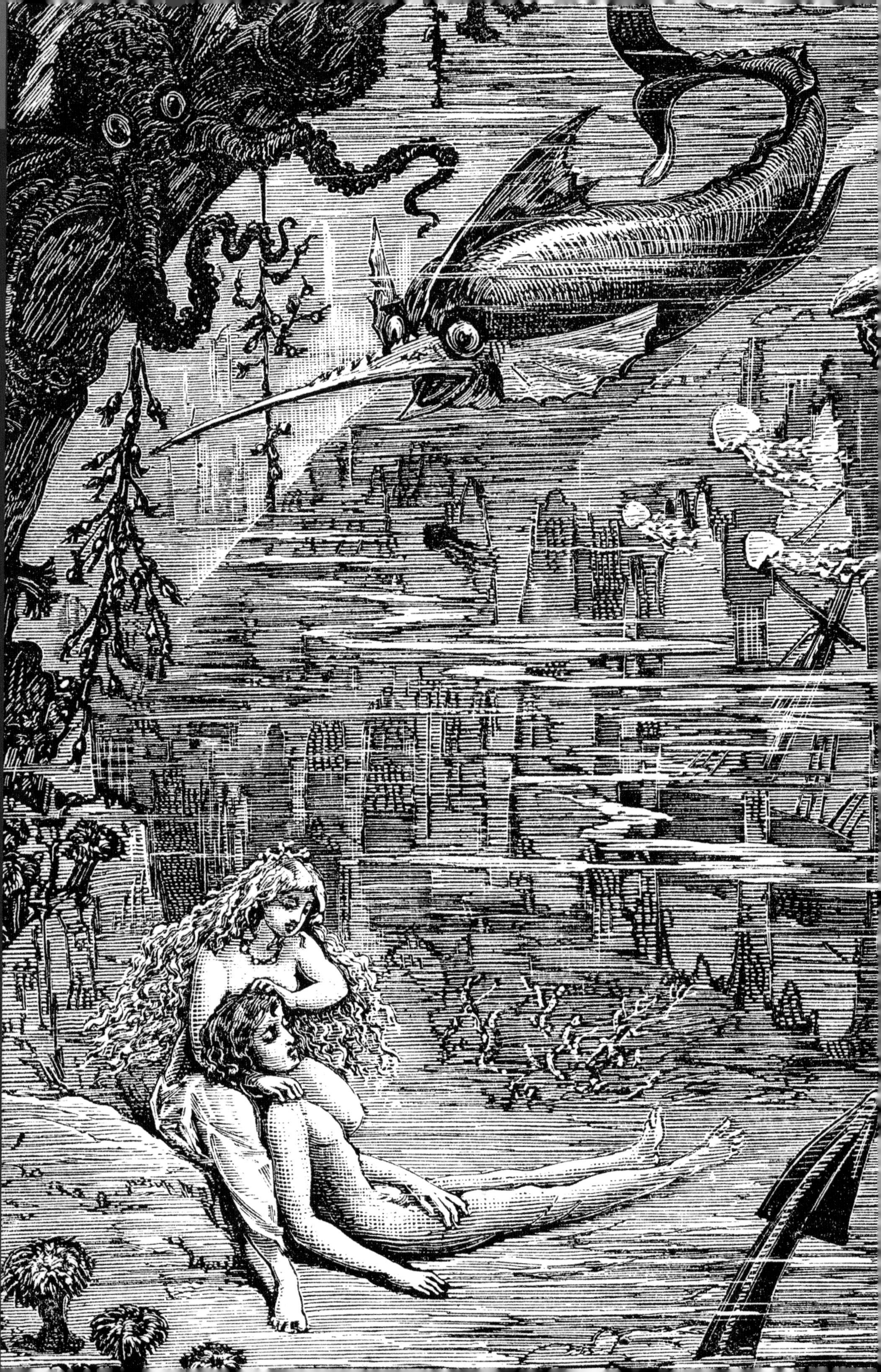

Many mermaids are kind to humans. They keep sailors safe. But some mermaid relatives are wicked. They are blamed for sinking boats. Some are said to take humans as slaves.

British stories told of mermaids taking the shape of humans and living on land for years.

Mermaids have

beautiful voices. They love to sing. In some stories, mermaids can do magic and see the future. They can talk to other sea creatures. They can also calm or create storms at sea.

Some mermaids might use their singing to get sailors to jump overboard.

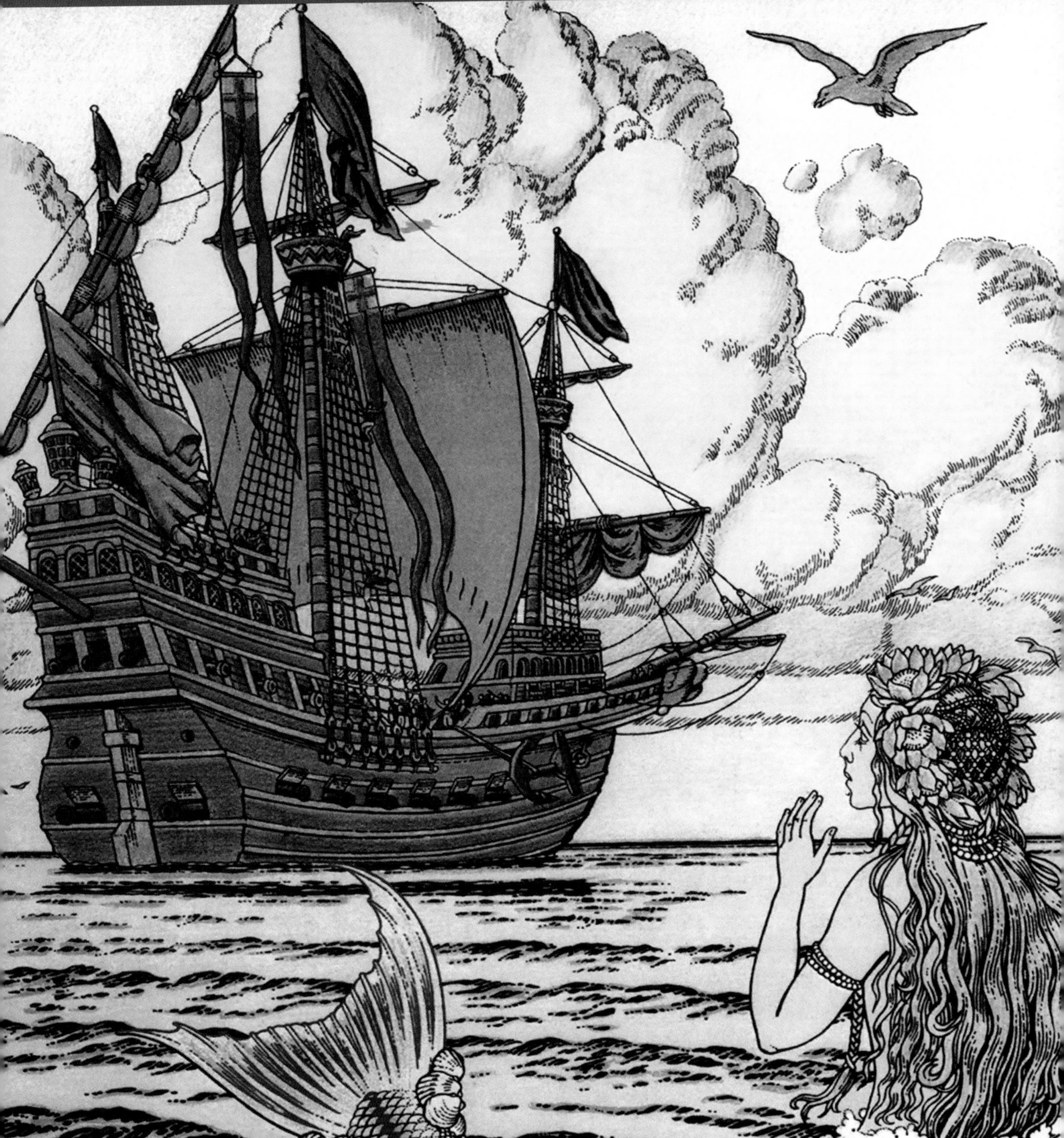

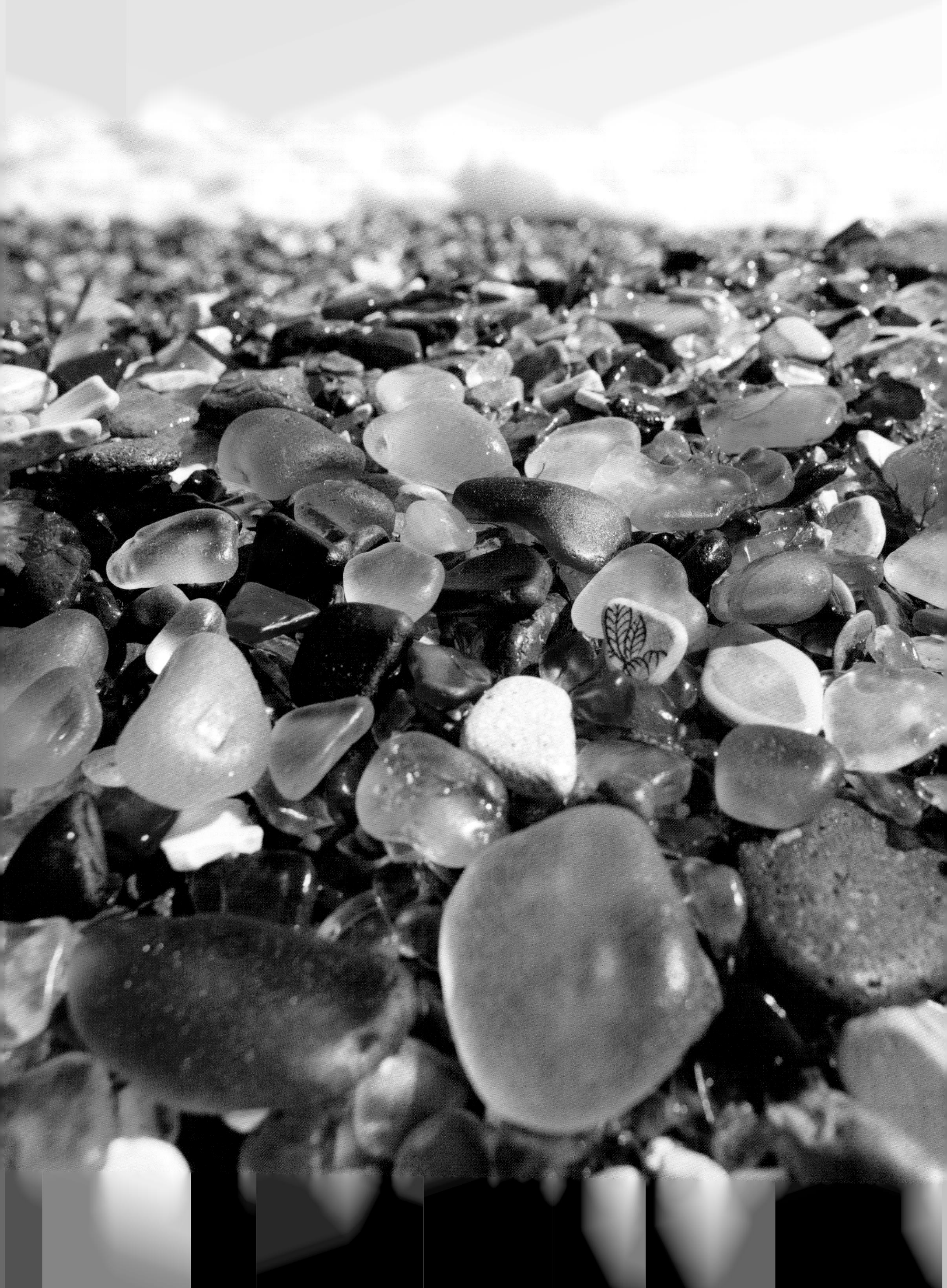

When mermaids cry, it is said their tears turn into sea glass. These beautiful stones wash up on beaches around the world. Some people believe mermaid tears bring good luck.

Sea glass actually comes from glass materials that have been worn smooth by water and sand.

Today, many people pretend to be mermaids. They wear costumes and swim underwater. Some clubs and recreation centers even offer mermaid-swimming lessons for kids!

Swimming with a mermaid tail can be a fun challenge!

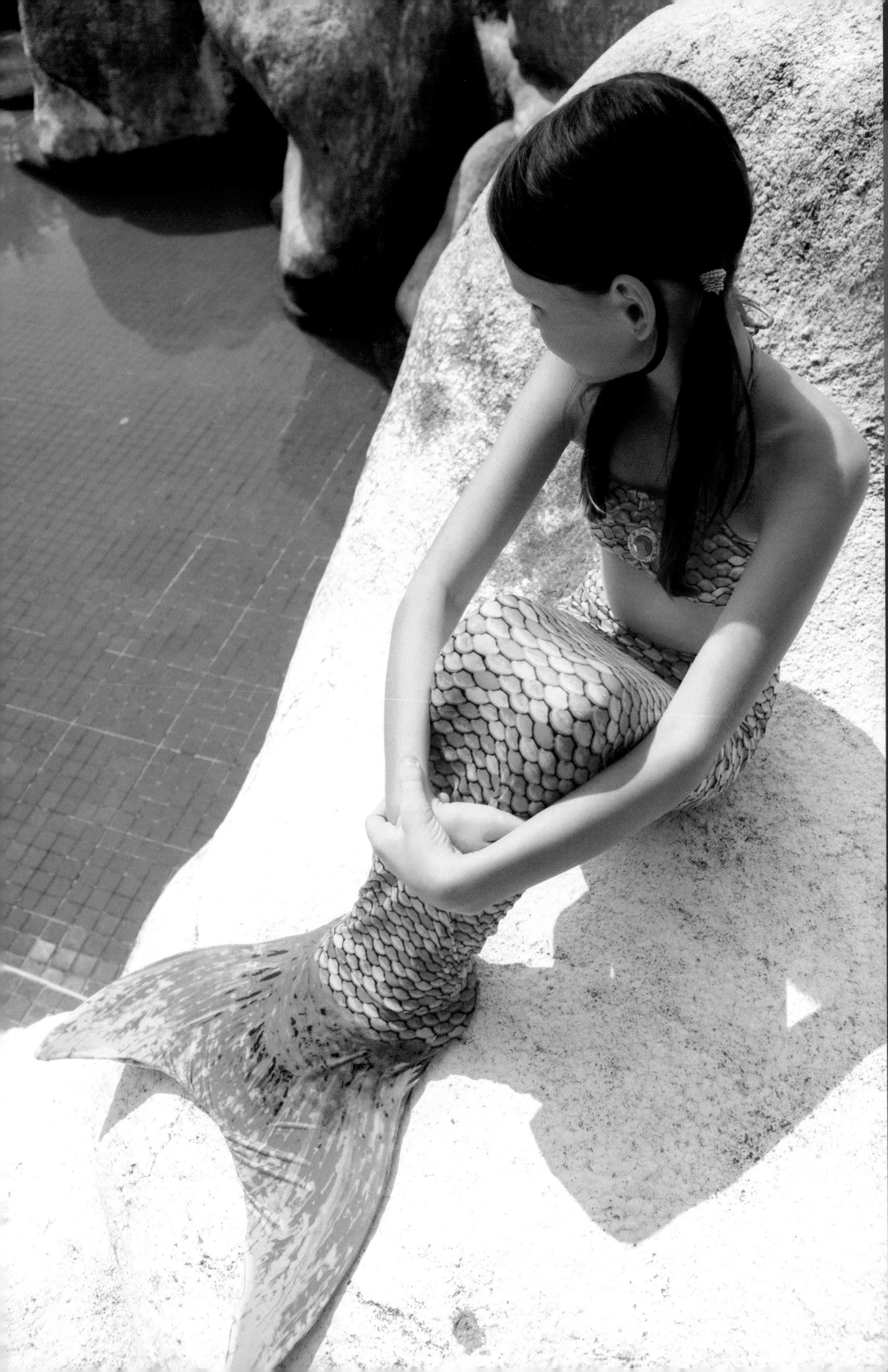

A Mermaid Story

One day, a mermaid stranded on the beach saw an old beggar on the shore. If he captured her, he could sell her and become rich. The mermaid was afraid. But the old man was kind. He carried her to the water. As a reward, the mermaid turned him into a young man. Now the man could have a new life. Perhaps he would become rich on his own!

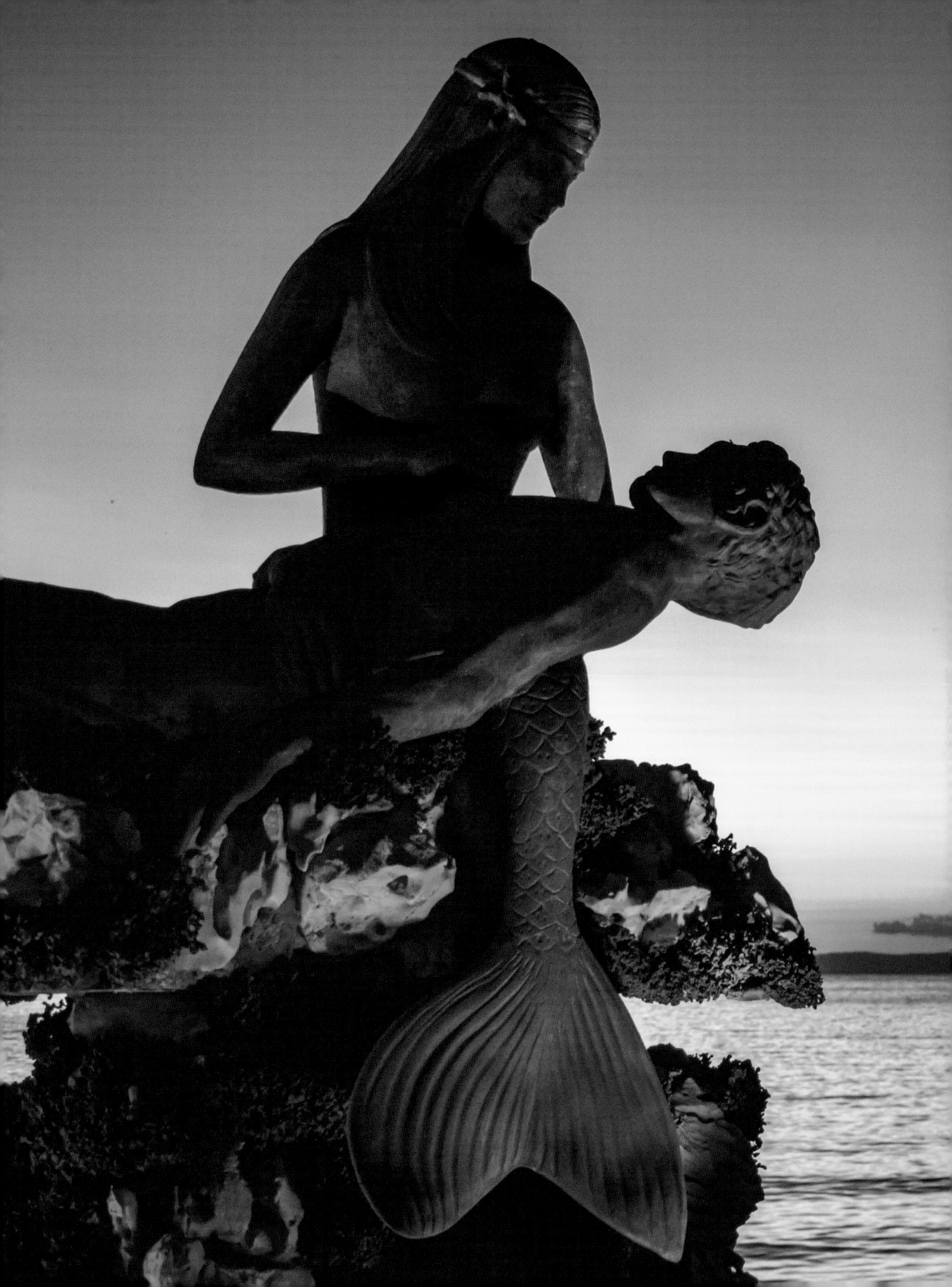

Read More

Alberti, Theresa Jarosz. *Mermaids*. Mendota Heights, Minn.: Focus Readers, 2019.

Grandi, Gina L. *The Magic of Mermaids*. New York: Downtown Bookworks, 2019.

Summers, Portia, and Dana Meachen Rau. *Are Mermaids Real?* New York: Enslow, 2017.

Websites

FinFriends: Are Mermaids Real?
https://www.finfriends.com/mermaids-real/
This site seeks to answer the question!

KidzSearch: Mermaid
https://wiki.kidzsearch.com/wiki/mermaid
Learn more about merfolk of the world.

Note: Every effort has been made to ensure that the websites listed above are suitable for children, that they have educational value, and that they contain no inappropriate material. However, because of the nature of the Internet, it is impossible to guarantee that these sites will remain active indefinitely or that their contents will not be altered.

Index